THE STICKYBEARS' SCARY NIGHT

by Richard Hefter

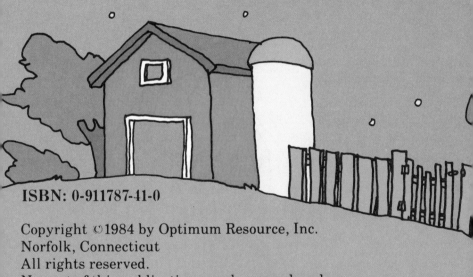

ISBN: 0-911787-41-0

THE STICKYBEARS' SCARY NIGHT

by Richard Hefter

Optimum Resource, Inc. Norfolk CT

It was just past supper time on a cold and windy evening.

Outside, the leaves shook and the windows rattled.

Inside the little house on Bushy Hill Road, it was cozy and warm.

Sara and Bedford Stickybear were helping their son, Bumper, get ready for bed.

"Dad," said Bumper, "I don't like the dark. I can't see at night and I get a little scared."

"Brush your teeth," said Stickybear, "and then put on your pajama top.

"You don't have to worry about the dark; it is good and very friendly. There is nothing to be afraid of at night."

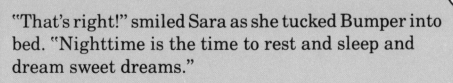

"That's right!" smiled Sara as she tucked Bumper into bed. "Nighttime is the time to rest and sleep and dream sweet dreams."

Then, Stickybear and Sara bent over the bed and gave Bumper a big kiss.

"Good night," they whispered as they turned off the light and tip-toed out of the room.

Bumper rolled over. Then, he rolled over again. He squeezed his eyes shut tightly and tried to fall asleep.

Bumper heard a train in the distance. Then, he heard a truck roll past the house.

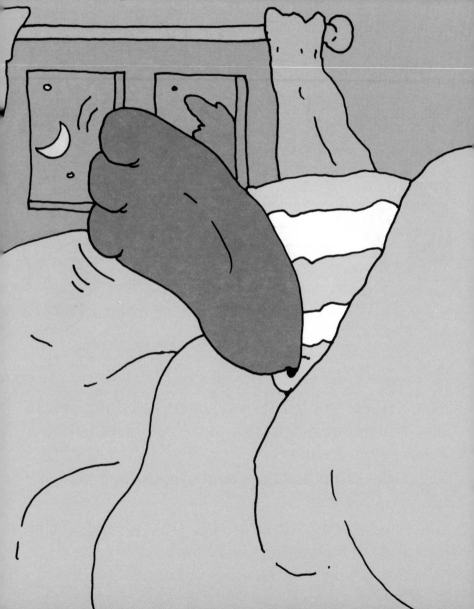

One of Bumper's feet stuck out of the blanket at the bottom of the bed. The foot got cold. The other foot stayed under the blanket and felt too hot.

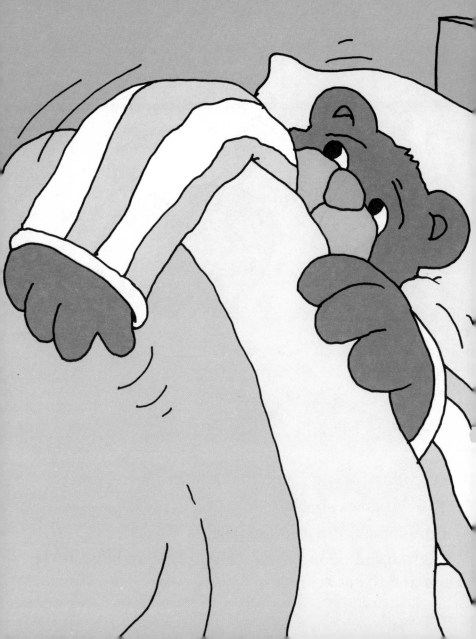

Outside, the wind whistled and howled.

The windows shook.

Bumper could not fall asleep.

He thought about terrible creatures and ghosts. He started to get scared.

He heard a squeak.
Then he heard a thump.
Squeak! Thump! Squeak! Thump!

"Help!" cried Bumper. "They're after me!"
He jumped right out of his bed. He ran all the way
down the hall and hopped into bed with Stickybear
and Sara.
"I'm scared," shivered Bumper. "There's a ghost or
something right outside my room going squeak,
thump!"

They hugged Bumper and walked him back to his room. Stickybear turned on the light.

"Look," smiled Stickybear. "There's nothing here but your bed and the chair and the table and your toys."

Stickybear looked under the table.
Then, he looked behind the bed.
"It's all right, Bumper," he said. "You don't have to
be afraid."

Just then, they all heard a loud SQUEAK and then a THUMP.

"You see," wailed Bumper, "they are here!"

Sara walked over to the window and looked out. She saw the fence. The gate was swinging back and forth in the wind. It made a squeaking, thumping noise.

"There is your ghost!" smiled Sara. "Someone left the gate open."

Bumper sighed. "I guess it was silly to get so scared," he said. "I'll try to go to sleep now."

Bumper climbed into his bed and pulled up the covers.

Stickybear and Sara went back to their room.
"I'd better go out and close the gate," said Stickybear,
"before the noise wakes up little Bumper again!"

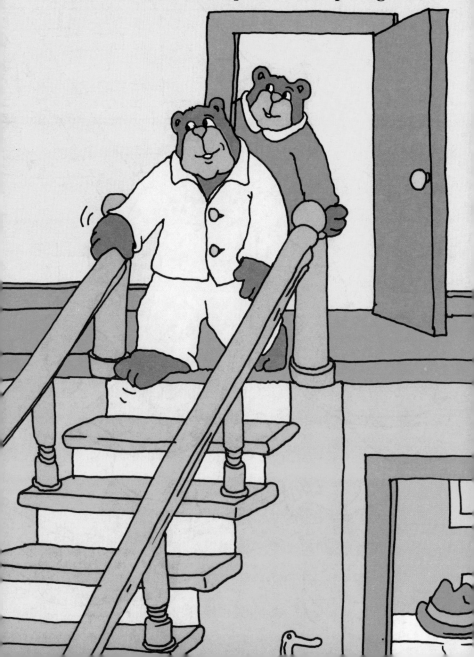

Stickybear went downstairs.
He put on his boots and his coat.
He reached for his hat.

His hat was gone!

Just then, he heard a CRASH in the kitchen!

Stickybear turned around and saw a strange white shape come from under the table.
The shape seemed to be wearing his hat.
It was moving fast.

"It's the ghost!" screeched Stickybear. "And it has my hat!"

Stickybear ran after the ghost.
The ghost jumped over the table.
Stickybear jumped over the table.

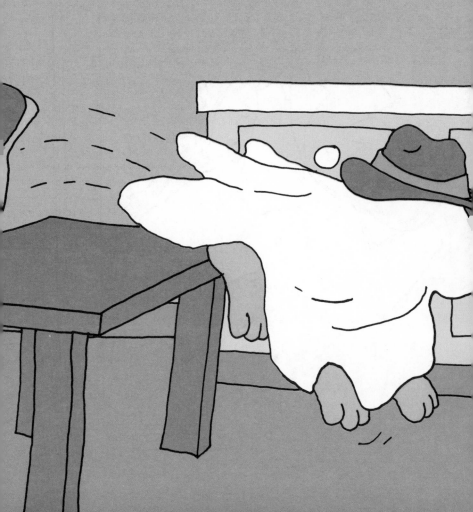

The ghost ran out the door!
Stickybear ran out the door!

The ghost ran behind the house.
Stickybear ran behind the house.

Bumper jumped out of bed and ran to the window. He looked out.

"Look," he shouted. "Dad is running after something scary!"

Sara rushed outside to help Stickybear.

Around and around the yard they ran.

Sara ran after Stickybear.
Stickybear ran after the ghost.
The ghost ran away with the hat.

"Stop!" puffed Stickybear. "Give me back my hat!"

The ghost ran over to the barn.
Stickybear ran faster and faster.
Sara ran after Stickybear.
Bumper looked out the window.

The ghost stopped suddenly!
Stickybear bumped into it and tumbled over.
Sara bumped into Stickybear.

They all fell in a heap!
The hat fell off the ghost.
The tablecloth fell off, too.

"Look at that!" laughed Sara. "Your 'ghost' was just the dog."

"Woof," barked the dog.

They all went back inside the house.
The dog curled up by the fireplace.
Stickybear and Sara went back upstairs.

Bumper climbed up into his bed again. He pulled the covers up around his ears.

"My," he yawned, "this surely has been a scary night."

Bumper smiled a little bear smile and snuggled down in his pillow.

In a few minutes, he was snoring a little bear snore and was fast asleep.